Richard was a Picker

WRITTEN BY
CaroLyn Beck

ILLUSTRATED BY
Ben Hodson

ORCA BOOK PUBLISHERS

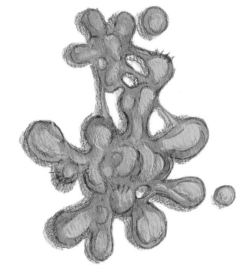

To M., who picked me.
—C.B.

To my adorable daughter, Zoe.
May this story never happen to you.
—B.H.

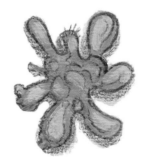

He'd stick his finger up his snout
and prod and pry and scoop stuff out.
He stretched the gooey slimy strings
into loops and swingy things.

From the crumbles, gobs and ooze
he sculpted castles, farms and ZOOS.

Jelly yellows and gooky whites
made robots, trains and satellites.
Globby browns and clabbery greens
built airports, towns and SUBMARINES.

Then One day

as he dug about,
Richard's finger would **NOT** come out!

He pulled, he tugged,
he grasped and gripped,
but up, up, **UP**
his finger slipped!

One knuckle,
  two knuckles,
    then all three.
      "Oh, no," said Richard.
        "How can thith be?"

He tried a yank, a jerk, a twist.
In went his hand up to his wrist!
"Help!" he honked in puzzled alarm.
SNORT!
Richard's nose sucked up his arm.

Richard froze.
He dared not blink,
    or gasp,
        or twitch,
            or even **ThiNK!**

Around him fell the strangest hush.

Then, rumble! **GRUMBLe!**

WHOOSH

WUUUUSH

WUSH!

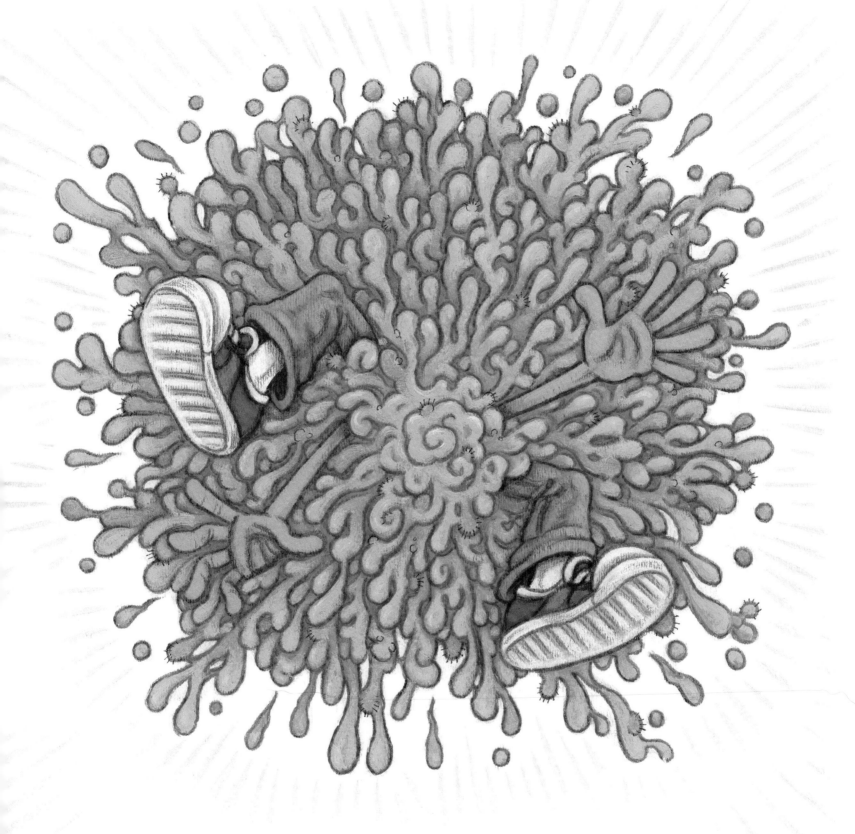

Shoulders, chest, knees and toes—
the rest of Richard slid **UP his NOSe.**

Richard was **iN**
his half-picked snout,
which now was **COMPLETELY**
iNSide OUT.
He looked like a booger,
a big gloopy blob,
an ooey, gluey, goobery **gLOB.**

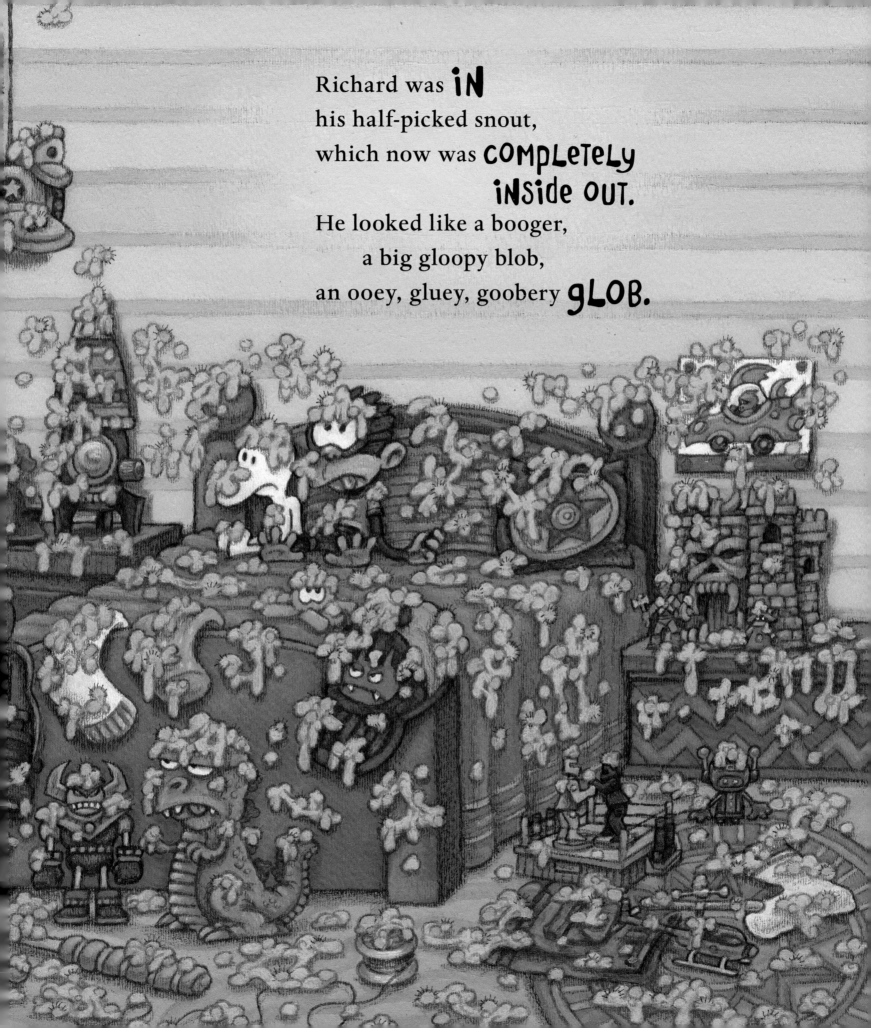

"HeLp! HeLp! HeLp!"
Richard's hollers were so muffled,
    so wee,
they couldn't be heard by even
      a FLea.

He wriggled his fingers and squiggled his toes.
But still he stayed STUCK
inside his nose.

He wormed. He squirmed.
He snapped and bumped.
He kicked. He flicked.
He flapped and thumped.

Then, with a shudder and a Sh-Sh-Shake,
Richard's inside-out snout began to quake.

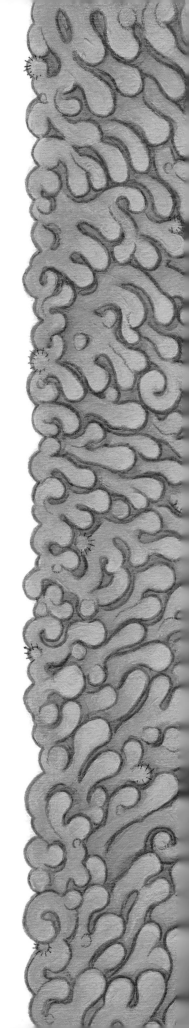

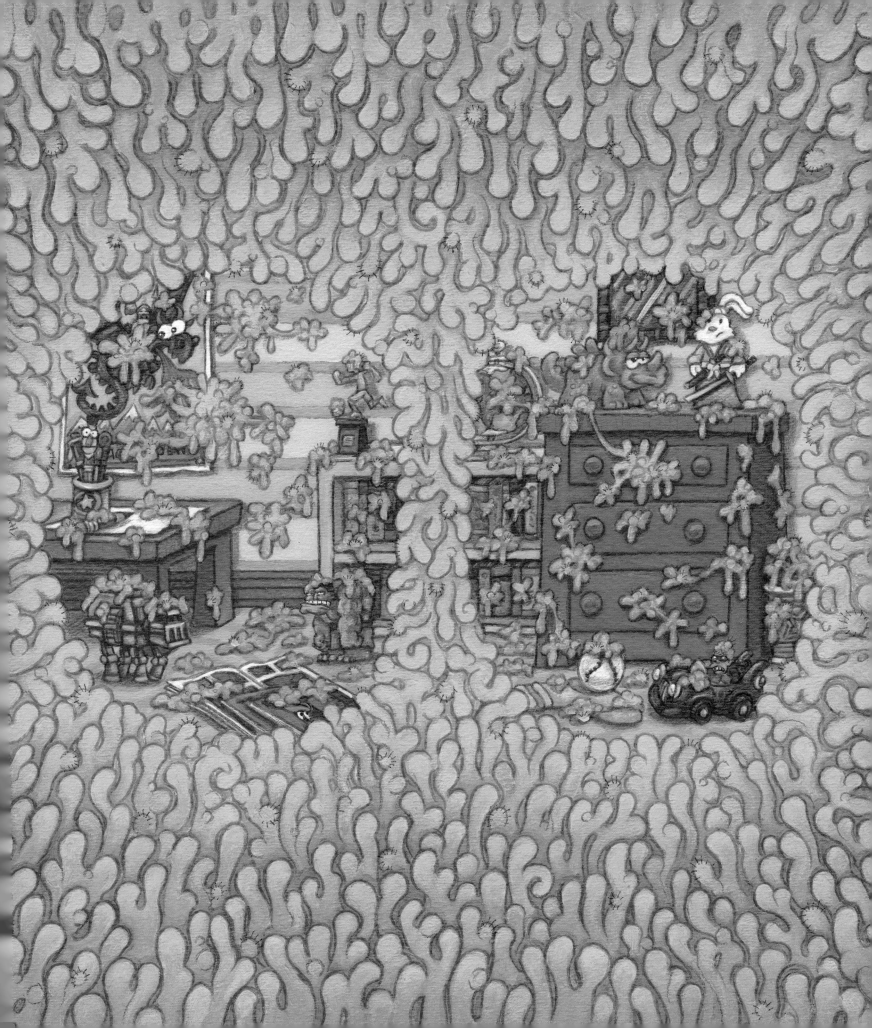

It wobbled and bobbled, tottered and rocked.
"To Ed's! To Ed's! To Ed's!" Richard squawked.

He zigged and z-z-zagged toward the door.
His GOOKY nose gathered stuff from the floor:
a book, a puzzle, the rug, a shoe,
a ball, some shorts, and a sock or two.

He rumbled, he tumbled down the hall.
Pictures fell from their hooks on the wall.
As he lurched from his house into the street,
he bowled his mother RighT OFF heR FeeT.

He picked up six cats, five crows, one mouse,
an unsuspecting dog sleeping in his house,
a wagon, a frog, two babies in a pool
and old Mrs. Rappertaffy knitting on her stool.
Neighbors yelled. Neighbors ran.
Richard kept on rolling.
He had a plan!

He rolled past the bank and Morrie's Meats,
by Flora's Flowers and Stella's Sweets.
Behind him chased the entire town.
"Catch it!" they cried. "Hunt that thing down!"
They waved canes and sticks
and big wooden spoons,
chains and picks
and nasty harpoons.

But Richard kept rolling.
He was headed for Ed's.
If he didn't make it,
he'd be SHREDDED
TO SHREDS!

"GET THOSE BABIES! STOP THAT BLOB!"
The crowd chasing Richard was a mad, mad mob!

Four blocks.
Three blocks.
Just two blocks to go.
But Richard's snout
was beginning to SLOW.

His nose was **TOO** loaded,
TOO lumped and clumped.
Seeing their chance, the six cats jumped.
Five crows flew, one mouse leapt
while the dog in his house slept and slept.

With one block left Richard slowed to a crawl.
He was barely moving at all,

AT aLL.

Then came the jab
of a big wooden spoon
and the quick sharp prick
of a rusty harpoon.

Richard bumped to a stone-dead stop
directly in front of Ed's Spice Shop.
"GET iT! BASH iT! MASH iT!" cried the horde.
"NET iT! THRASH iT! SMASH iT!" they roared.

"ST-ST-STOP!" stammered Richard.
"STOP! STOP! PLEASE!"
He crossed his fingers and waited for a
"AH...

...AAAH-AAH-CHOOOOOOO!"

It could have been the parsley, the pepper, the thyme,
the nutmeg, the mustard, the ginger or the lime.
It could have been the cumin, the coriander, the salt.
The only thing that mattered
was the **eNd ReSULT.**

The babies, the wagon, the socks, the frog,
the pictures, the puzzle, the rug, the dog,
the book, the ball, the shorts, the shoe,
old Mrs. Rappertaffy
and Richard too—

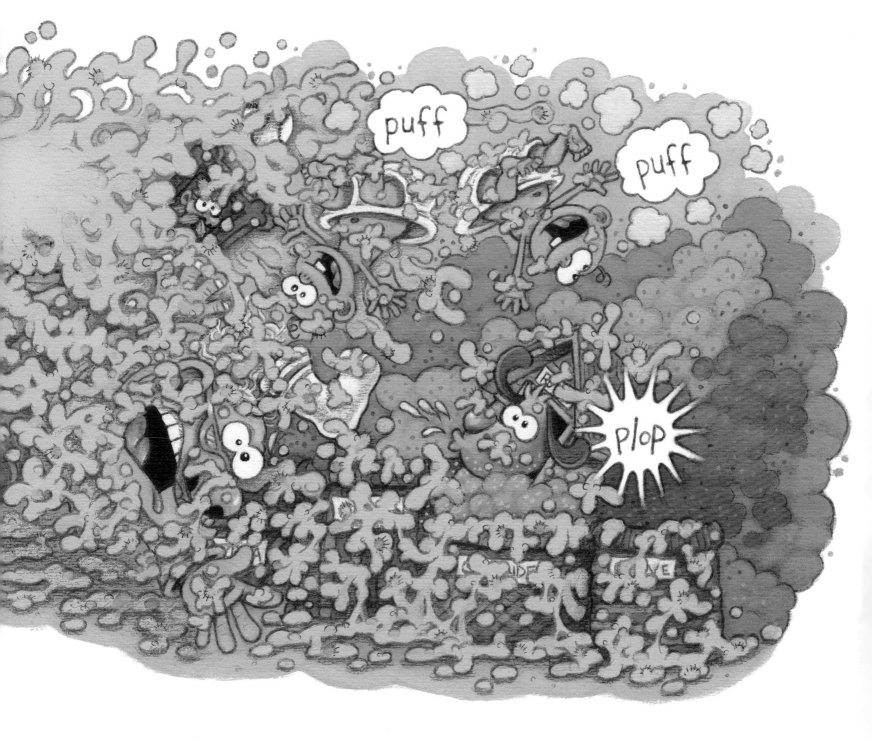

EVERYTHING went flipping
and flying round and round,
but all landed safely
on a soft, spicy mound.
The babies went **PUFF.** The dog went **PLOP.**
Old Mrs. Rappertaffy went **FLIP, FLAP, FLOP!**

The crowd stood astounded. They were plastered in snot.
"B-Booger Boy?!" they spluttered. "That's YOU, is it not?"

Richard rubbed his nose. It was very, very sore.
"BOOGER BOY?" he said. "No. That's not me.

NOT ANYMORE."

Library and Archives Canada Cataloguing in Publication

Beck, Carolyn
Richard was a picker / written by Carolyn Beck ; illustrated by Ben Hodson.

Also available in an electronic format.
ISBN 978-1-55469-088-6

I. Hodson, Ben II. Title.
PS8553.E2949R53 2010   JC813'.6   C2010-903514-3

First published in the United States, 2010
Library of Congress Control Number: 2010928728

Summary: Richard's nose-picking leads to trouble when he gets sucked up inside his own nose and can't get out.

sniff

Mixed Sources
Cert no. SW-COC-001271
© 1996 FSC
FSC

Orca Book Publishers is dedicated to preserving the environment and has printed this book on paper certified by the Forest Stewardship Council.

Orca Book Publishers gratefully acknowledges the support for its publishing programs provided by the following agencies: the Government of Canada through the Canada Book Fund and the Canada Council for the Arts, and the Province of British Columbia through the BC Arts Council and the Book Publishing Tax Credit.

Interior and cover artwork created using acrylic paint and colored pencil on watercolor paper.
Design by Teresa Bubela

ORCA BOOK PUBLISHERS
PO BOX 5626, STN. B
VICTORIA, BC CANADA
V8R 6S4

ORCA BOOK PUBLISHERS
PO BOX 468
CUSTER, WA USA
98240-0468

www.orcabook.com
Printed and bound in Canada.

13 12 11 10 • 4 3 2 1